There Was A Crooked Man

Retold by
Russell Punter

Illustrated by David Semple

Reading consultant: Alison Kelly
Roehampton University

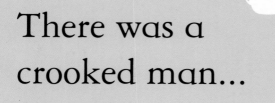

There was a crooked man...

...and he walked a crooked mile.

He found a crooked
sixpence...

...upon a crooked stile.

He bought a
crooked cat...

...which caught a crooked mouse.

And they all lived together...

...in a little
crooked house.

The crooked man
was hungry.

So he cooked a
crooked fish.

His crooked cat
could smell it.

And she snatched it
off the dish.

The crooked man
was angry.

He chased his cat
outside.

He couldn't see her
anywhere.

She'd found a place
to hide.

The man smelled
something fishy.

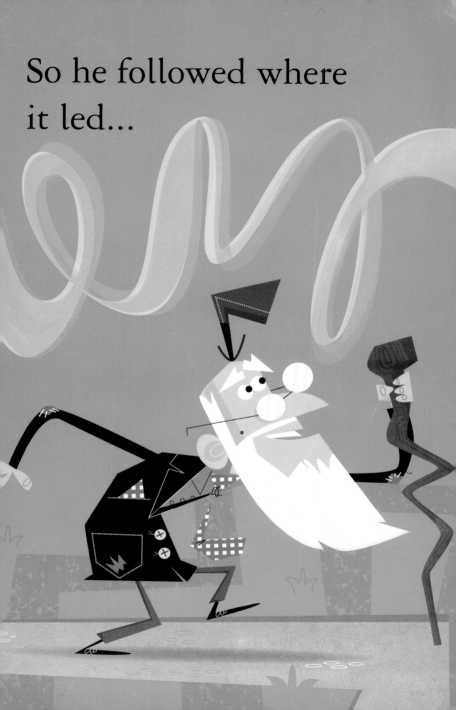

So he followed where
it led...

...across his crooked garden...

...into his crooked shed.

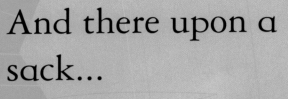

And there upon a
sack...

...snuggled up against
each other...

...were thirteen
hungry kittens...

...and their kind but crooked mother.

PUZZLES

Puzzle 1

Can you spot the differences between these two pictures? There are six to find.

27

Puzzle 2
Find these things in the picture:

cat   fish   dish

hat   chair   window

Puzzle 3
Choose the best sentence in each picure.

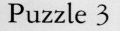

I'm angry.

I'm hungry.

Give it back!

Give it away!

Answers to puzzles

Puzzle 1

Puzzle 2

window — hat

cat

chair

dish — fish

Puzzle 3

About the story

There Was A Crooked Man is based on an old nursery rhyme. It was written about a Scottish General named Sir Alexander Leslie.

Series editor:
Lesley Sims

First published in 2009 by Usborne Publishing Ltd., Usborne House,
83-85 Saffron Hill, London EC1N 8RT, England. www.usborne.com
Copyright © 2009 Usborne Publishing Ltd.

USBORNE FIRST READING
Level Three

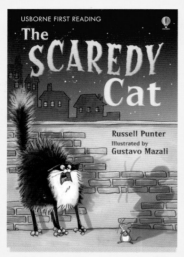

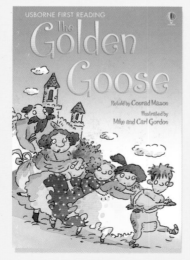